TONY HICKEY

Flip 'n' Flop
and the movies

Illustrated by Terry Myler

THE CHILDREN'S PRESS

First published 1997 by
The Children's Press
an imprint of Anvil Books
45 Palmerston Road, Dublin 6

ISBN 1 901737 05 5

*Dedicated to
animal-movie lovers everywhere*

Typeset by Computertype Limited
Printed by Colour Books Limited

Contents

1   What's Going on?   7

2   On the Run!   13

3   The Hotel   23

4   Thunder   29

5   Talking to a Dog Star   35

6   Dave Adams   45

7   Harry the Trainer   56

8   Detectives   68

9   Shoe Hunt   78

10 Sniffing Around   86

11 Thunder to the Rescue   94

12 Action and Happy Endings   107

1

What's Going On?

Flip and Flop lay under the dark-green bushes that grew around the cottage. With them was Topsy, the sheep-dog, who lived on the next farm with Bart O'Sullivan. Topsy always called at the cottage first thing in the morning.

They heard the sound of something moving through the bracken at the top of the path to the beach. A cat that Flip and Flop had never seen before came into view.

'Good morning,' the cat said.

'Oh it's you,' said Topsy, lying down again. 'What brings you all the way out from the town so early in the morning?'

'I've come to meet the newcomers,' said the cat.

She reminded Flip and Flop of Catriona, the cat who used to come and talk to them when they lived in Killiney.

'You can hardly call them newcomers. They've been here for months now,' Topsy said crossly. He didn't sound as though he liked the cat very much.

'We still must be polite to each other,' purred the cat.

'Oh very well,' growled Topsy. 'These are my friends, Flip and Flop, who live here with Frank and Lucy. This is Silky, the cat.'

The border terriers nodded in greeting at Silky.

Silky smiled back and said, 'In case you are wondering why I am called "Silky", it is because of my coat. It is exactly like silk to touch.'

Before the terriers could think of what to say to this, the cottage door opened. Lucy gave a loud scream and rushed out into the morning sunlight.

'No, no,' she cried. 'You will not take my dogs away from me. No matter what you say or do, I will not let you take my dogs away!'

Frank ran out after her. He waved his arms and shouted, 'Those dogs are dangerous animals and have to be got rid of!' Then he grabbed Lucy by the arm, dragged her back into the cottage and slammed the door.

Silky looked at Flip and Flop. She said,

'It sounds to me as though Frank wants to get rid of you!'

'That can't be true,' said Flop. 'Frank loves us.'

'And so does Lucy,' added Flip.

'Shh!' Silky held her paw up for silence. She put her head against the door of the cottage and listened.

'What is it?' whispered Flop.

'They still seem to be arguing,' said Silky. Then she jumped away from the door. 'Quick! We'd better hide. They are coming out again.' The three dogs and Silky ran in among the trees close to the cottage.

Frank and Lucy threw the front door open. Lucy rushed towards the road. Then she turned back and shouted, 'You will never take my dogs away from me. Never! Never!'

Frank waved his arms again and yelled, 'I will, I will, I will! If it is the last thing I do, I will get rid of those brutes!' Then he threw his arms around Lucy. 'They will get a great surprise when they start to shoot dogs out here.' They both roared with laughter.

Flip could feel Flop trembling all over.

9

Then he realised that he was trembling as well. So too was Topsy. Silky didn't move at all. She sat like a small statue, watching the two humans.

Lucy stopped laughing and said, 'I wonder where Flip and Flop are. I hope they haven't gone wandering off.' She looked around but didn't notice the animals in among the trees.

Frank glanced at his watch. 'We're going to be late for the meeting if we don't hurry.' He whistled his usual whistle for the dogs.

The dogs crouched down as low as they could.

'Maybe they've gone to the beach with Topsy,' said Lucy.

'I don't like leaving them out on their own.' Frank sounded worried.

'Oh they may as well enjoy themselves while they can,' said Lucy. 'We can take care of them when we get back.'

'Yes, I suppose we can,' agreed Frank. 'Bart O'Sullivan will help us to find them.'

Then Lucy and Frank locked the cottage door and drove off.

'I can't believe my ears,' said Topsy. 'They're planning to get rid of you.'

'For all we know Mr O'Sullivan might be planning the same thing for you,' said Flip.

'But why do they want to get rid of us?' asked Flop. 'What did we do wrong?'

The three dogs felt so sad that they threw back their heads and keened.

Almost at once they heard Jer, who lived with the O'Sheas, keen back.

Then the great deep voice of Plucky, the wolf-hound, called out, 'What is it? What's wrong?'

'It's Frank and Lucy,' Flop howled back. 'They want to get rid of us.'

'And Bart O'Sullivan might want to get rid of me too,' howled Topsy.

'Maybe the humans are going to get rid of all us dogs,' howled Flip.

'Stuff and nonsense!' said Mitch, the donkey. The dogs had been making so much noise that they hadn't heard him galloping across the fields. Now he was looking at them over the hedge.

'You didn't hear what we just heard,' said Topsy. He led the border terriers and Silky out from among the trees. Quickly he told the donkey everything. Jer and Plucky arrived in time to hear most of it too.

'There must be some mistake,' said Plucky. 'There just has to be some mistake.'

' A mistake often leads dogs astray. And that's a well-known fact,' said Jer.

'There is definitely something wrong here,' said Silky.

'Of course there is something wrong!' said Topsy. 'The humans are planning to get rid of us. That's what's wrong.'

Silky said, ' We need more information. I should get back to the town as quickly as possible. Maybe I can find out what this meeting that Frank mentioned is all about.'

'Hop up on my back and I'll get you there in a few minutes,' said Mitch.

'Flop and I are coming too,' said Flip.

'And what are the rest of us going to do?' asked Topsy.

'Wait here until we get back,' said Silky. Then Mitch galloped off across the fields, with Silky on his back and Flip and Flop running alongside.

2

On the Run!

When they reached the edge of the town, Mitch said to the terriers, 'Just in case there is something wrong, why don't the two of you wait for me down at the river?'

Flip and Flop ran along the river bank until they came to a clump of trees. 'No one will see us here,' Flop said.

The wind carried rain in from the sea. The day was becoming grey and cold. Flip and Flop huddled together.

After a while Flip said, 'Maybe we should think of trying to get back to Killiney. We'd be safe there.'

'Yes,' said Flop. 'If we knew for sure in which direction Killiney is.'

'Hey, cheer up!' Silky was sitting on a branch of one of the trees.

'You found us!'

'Mitch told me that you were here,' Silky said. 'He's staying close to the road for a few more seconds to make sure that no one from the town followed me.'

'Did you find out anything about the

13

strangers wanting to shoot us?' asked Flop.

'Yes. That was what the meeting at the hotel was about,' said Silky. 'But they are not just going to shoot dogs. They are going to shoot Lucy too.'

'That must be because she tried to stop Frank from getting rid of us this morning,' said Flip.

'No, it's because she is an actor,' said the cat. 'There's a film company in the town to make a movie. The name of the movie is *Dogs*. And Lucy has got a part in it! When we heard Lucy and Frank going on about getting rid of dogs this morning, they were rehearsing a scene from the film.'

'What's "rehearsing"?' Flop asked.

'It's trying out how something sounds or looks,' said Silky. 'Lucy wanted to get it right before she went to that special meeting this morning. Now she's got the part in the movie. And everyone for miles around is hoping to be in it. That's why all the humans went to the meeting in the hotel.'

'But do they still want to get rid of us dogs?' asked Flip. 'Do they still want to shoot us?'

'Of course they don't want to shoot you,'

14

exclaimed Silky. 'They want to shoot the film. A film is made up of hundreds of different "shots" or scenes. That's why they call it "shooting". Instead of being got rid of, the two of you could end up being in the movie.'

'And maybe Topsy and Jer and Plucky too,' said Flop. 'Let's go back and tell them the good news.'

Silky said, 'I'm afraid that I have some other very important things to attend to right now.'

Then she seemed to just vanish into the hedge.

Flip said, 'I wish cats didn't do that.'

They ran back to Mitch, who was as pleased at the good news as they were.

'We'll meet you at the cottage in a few minutes,' said Flip.

'Aren't you going to come back with me?' asked the donkey.

'Well now that we are not in any danger, I thought that we would see what's happening in the town,' said Flip.

Before Flop could stop him, Flip was running in the direction of the main street. 'I'd better go with him,' said Flop. 'Just in case he gets into any trouble.'

Flip and Flop kept very close to the walls of the shops and the houses. That way they hoped to avoid being seen by Garda Ryan. He didn't like animals on their own on the main street.

As it turned out they had no need to worry. All the humans and Garda Ryan were crowding around a large poster.

Before Flop could stop him, Flip had pushed his way through the crowd. His tail tickled several people, making them jump,

16

but Flip didn't notice this. He was too busy staring at the poster.

The poster was of a very handsome dog with the shiniest coat and biggest eyes that Flip had ever seen. The smile on the dog's face was more like a human smile than a dog smile. In big letters underneath were the words:

THUNDER, THE DOG THAT WOKE UP
THE WORLD!
THUNDER, THE NEW MOVIE SENSATION!

Thunder must be the star of the movie.

Flip called out, 'Flop! Flop! Come here quickly.'

To Flop it sounded as though Flip was in trouble.

'I'm coming,' he yelled. When he reached the front of the crowd and saw that Flip was all right he said very crossly, 'Why did you call me like that? I thought you were in trouble again.'

'I wanted you to see this poster,' Flip said.

Flop was just as amazed as Flip by it.

Garda Ryan said, 'I didn't know a dog was going to be the star.'

'And what is wrong with a dog being a movie star?' asked Flip.

But Garda Ryan didn't see Flip. Instead he and the other humans went back to their work, leaving the terriers all alone in front of the poster.

Or so they thought until they saw a woman in a red coat watching them.

She smiled. It was a lovely smile. In fact it was very like the smile on Thunder's face. The dogs couldn't help wagging their tails at her.

'Oh, so you are friendly,' she said in a strange accent. 'Maybe you and I could be friends?'

Friends! Flip and Flop had forgotten that they were supposed to be bringing the good news to their own friends. They had to go.

'Hey, what's your hurry?' the woman called after them. 'I'm Jenny Lewis from America. I'm working on the movie.'

'We must go back and talk to her some other time,' said Flip.

The two terriers did not slow down until they got to the cottage.

The rain had stopped. The wind had

dropped. Bright sunshine made the ocean sparkle once more.

The waiting dogs were delighted to hear that they were not going to be got rid of.

'I'm too old to go wandering around the countryside looking for somewhere new to live,' said Plucky.

'But you might not be too old to get a part in the movie,' laughed Flip.

'We might all end up in the movies. And that's a well-known fact,' cried Jer.

That thought made the dogs feel so happy and dizzy that they half-ran, half-danced down to the beach and back to the cottage.

Frank and Lucy were home by now. Frank came out and said, 'Hey, hey! Keep the noise down. We have visitors.'

The dogs looked into the cottage. Seated at the kitchen table, drinking tea, were Jenny Lewis and a grey-haired man.

'Oh, so we meet again,' Jenny said to Flip and Flop. 'You are two very cute little dogs. So are your friends. And I'd like you to meet Martin O'Brien, one of the best movie directors, not just in Ireland but in the world.'

'Oh now, now...' said Martin.

'No, it's true! Why else would I come all the way from America to work with you?' said Jenny. 'That first movie you made with Thunder was a great success. This new one will be even bigger!'

Bigger? The dogs looked at each other. How could one movie be bigger than another? Then they realised that when Jenny said 'bigger' she meant it would make more money because more people would go and see it.

They learned many other things as well. They learned that Jenny was called a 'producer'. She worked for the big American company that was giving Martin the money to make the new Thunder movie.

It also seemed that Irish films were now loved by people all over the world. There were many very popular Irish movie stars and Thunder was the first Irish dog star!

Jenny said, 'We've just got to fit these mutts into the story too.'

Mutts! Flip and Flop didn't very much like being called 'mutts'.

Then Jenny said, 'Maybe they could help Thunder to solve the mystery of the dead sheep.'

Dead sheep? There were going to be dead sheep in the movie? Wow! Suddenly Flip and Flop forgot about being called 'mutts'. The movie now sounded, not just exciting, but downright dangerous.

'There is one problem,' said Martin. 'I may not have time to rewrite the script.'

The dogs all groaned. So did all the humans. Then Jenny brightened up and said, 'Hey, just a minute. Frank, aren't you a writer?'

'Well, yes, I am,' said Frank.

'There you are.' Jenny slapped the table as she spoke. 'Why can't you help Martin rewrite the script? You understand dogs and their ways. It would make things much easier since you know the country-side too.'

'That's settled then,' said Martin.

'Now about us using this cottage in the movie,' Jenny said. 'You will have to live somewhere else for the next four weeks. We will pay your rent for you wherever you decide to go.'

'It would have to be somewhere that takes dogs,' said Lucy.

'What about the hotel in the town?' said

Martin. 'Thunder will be staying there. Flip and Flop would be company for him.'

'That's a great idea,' said Jenny. 'He will be arriving in the morning with Mrs Brennan, who looks after him. Could you move to the hotel that soon and start work on the script right away?'

'Yes, of course we can. When will you start filming?' asked Frank.

'In about four days' time. Harry, the trainer, could start working with the dogs before then,' said Martin.

'Let's all have breakfast at the hotel tomorrow,' suggested Jenny.

The dogs needed time to think. So much had happened so quickly. They slipped away to the green bushes at the side of the cottage.

'Where will Martin and Jenny get the dead sheep from?' asked Flip.

'Please don't ask questions like that,' said Flop as he tried to stop a new shiver from running down his spine.

3

The Hotel

Early next morning Frank and Lucy loaded up the car and drove into town, with Flip and Flop on the back seats.

When they arrived at the hotel car park Mr Skelly, the manager, rushed out to meet them.

'Ah good morning, good morning. Mr and Mrs Johnson, isn't it? Or perhaps Mrs Johnson uses her acting name, Lucy Crater?'

'Yes, I do when I am acting,' said Lucy. 'These are our dogs, Flip and Flop.'

Mr Skelly's smile faded. 'Oh yes. Miss Lewis said there would be your dogs. I had almost forgotten. But please why don't you and Mr Johnson go on into the dining-room? Miss Lewis and Mr O'Brien are waiting there to have breakfast with you.'

'What about the luggage and Flip and Flop?' asked Frank.

'Oh don't worry. I will attend to them.'

Flip and Flop didn't care for the way that Mr Skelly looked at them.

'No noise, please,' he said. 'Just get out of the car and SIT!'

The dogs did as they were told but not because they afraid of Mr Skelly. They didn't want to make trouble for Frank and Lucy.

Mr Skelly called, 'Seamus!'

Seamus hurried out into the car park. He was very tall and young looking. He was trying to put on a white jacket as he came towards Mr Skelly.

'No, no, Seamus, you don't need your white jacket now,' the manager said. 'I want you to take this luggage up to room seventeen for Mr and Mrs Johnson.'

'And what about the two dogs?' asked Seamus.

Just then Mr Skelly's mobile phone rang. As he answered it, his hand shook nervously. 'Hello ... I will attend to it right away myself. Problems in the kitchen.' He hurried into the hotel.

Seamus grinned at Flip and Flop. 'Don't mind Mr Skelly. He's a bit fussed because the hotel is so full with the film people.'

Flip and Flop sat in the cold yard and watched Seamus unload the car. When he took their basket out they decided to follow him into the hotel. He didn't seem to notice that they were right behind him.

He went up two flights of stairs and into a bedroom. He put the basket in the space between the bed and the window. Flip and Flop waited. After a few minutes Seamus came back with the last of the luggage. Then he went away without closing the door properly.

'I'm hungry,' said Flip.

'So am I,' said Flop.

'I think that I can smell something cooking,' said Flip. Maybe whoever is doing the cooking will give us something to eat. Let's go and find them.'

'Okay,' said Flop, forgetting to be nervous.

The two little terriers ran along the corridor. The smell came from downstairs. They stuck their heads through the banisters and listened. They could hear the sound of pots and pans behind swing doors. The doors opened. A man with four plates of delicious-smelling food on a tray passed directly underneath them.

'If we were down a few more steps we could have almost touched that food,' Flip said.

'That might not be such a good idea,' said Flop but Flip was already on the move.

He went down seven more steps and waited. The swing doors opened again. This time a woman came out, carrying another tray of food on plates. Flip swiped at them with his paw and missed.

'You have to be a cat to do that,' said a voice.

The terriers looked up. Silky was perched on the banister above their heads. Flop said, 'I didn't know that you lived in the hotel.'

'I don't live here,' said Silky. 'I just come and visit when I feel like it. I'm surprised to see the two of you here. Usually dogs aren't allowed in the hotel.'

'We are staying here,' said Flip. 'We are going to be in the movie.'

'I am thinking of being in it myself. That is if they offer me a big enough part,' said the cat. 'Would you like me to get you something to eat?'

The swing doors opened once more. Another man came out carrying another tray of food. He seemed to be having difficulty keeping the tray straight. He paused directly under the two dogs and tried to get a better grip of the tray.

Silky slid down the banister and with a flick of her tail knocked the tray out of the man's hand. 'Quick!' she said. 'Get moving!'

Without even thinking, Flip and Flop rushed down the stairs into the hall. Silky landed by the food at the same time as the terriers. They could hear human voices in the kitchen. Flip grabbed a sausage. Flop took a rasher and a fried egg. The swing doors opened. Two cooks and a waiter ran

out into the hall.

The waiter said, 'I knew he shouldn't have tried to carry that tray. It takes years to learn how to carry a tray properly.'

Flip and Flop realised that the man who had been carrying the tray was lying on the floor. It was Mr Skelly, the hotel manager! He opened his eyes and saw Flip and Flop.

'Those dogs did it,' he yelled. 'They tripped me up! Who let them into the hotel? Where is that Seamus?'

Flop tried to explain but Silky said, 'Save your breath and follow me.' She snatched a rasher from among the broken plates and ran into the dining-room.

Flip and Flop followed her, trying to eat and run at the same time. They didn't see the waitress until she fell over them and landed on the ground. Mr Skelly and the kitchen staff rushed in and fell over her too. A table got turned over as hotel guests stood up to see what was happening.

'Through the window,' yelled Silky.

It was a good thing that the window was open. Flip and Flop landed safely outside and ran as fast as they could after Silky.

4

Thunder

Silky led the dogs to a big dusty building. There was a smell of straw. 'We will be safe here for a while,' she said.

Flip looked around him. 'What is this place?'

'It used to be the stables when the hotel was a house,' said Silky. 'I'll go outside and see what's happening. Try and be quiet.'

The dust in the air made Flop sneeze. 'We are going to need a bath by the time we get out of here.'

Flip tried to get comfortable on a pile of old sacks. Then he said, 'Frank and Lucy must be furious with us.'

'And what about Jenny and Martin? They saw what happened as well,' said Flop. 'If only they hadn't all been having breakfast in the dining-room!'

'Do you think they will change their mind about letting us be in the movie?' asked Flop. 'Or, worse than that, not let Frank and Lucy have anything to do with it.'

'There's no need to worry.' Silky was

back in the stables. 'Jenny Lewis said that she thought that the chase through the dining-room was one of the most exciting things she had ever seen. She wants Frank and Martin to put it in the movie script.'

Flop had a sudden thought. 'Does that mean you're going to be in the movie as well?'

'Yes, Jenny insisted. She said the chase wouldn't be the same without me showing you two what to do. I'm to be the the only cat among all of you dogs. Mr Skelly is going to be in the movie too. He isn't angry with anyone any more. Thanks to me, all's well that ends well. Now, if you will excuse me, I have to go back to Mrs Shannon. I share a house in the market square with her. See you later on.' Then she seemed to just vanish into a cloud of dust.

Flip and Flop both shivered. 'I do wish that cats wouldn't do that,' said Flop. 'But they are very good at discovering things.'

There was the loud honking of a car horn. The terriers ran to the door.

A very stern-looking woman, with sleek black hair piled on top of her head, was getting out of the longest car that Flip and Flop had ever seen.

A driver in a blue uniform was holding the door of the car open.

Flop said, 'I think that woman might be Mrs Brennan.'

The driver went to the other side of the car and opened a door there. A large reddish-brown dog got out very slowly.

'That's Thunder,' said Flop. 'He looks just like his poster, only not quite so shiny.'

Thunder walked very slowly around the car and stared at Mrs Brennan, who wrapped her shawl tightly around herself and said, 'I'm not feeling at all well. I don't know why they couldn't wait until summer to make the movie. It's so cold here.'

Voices called out, 'Hello! Hello!' Jenny and Martin were hurrying across the yard. Mr Skelly followed, rubbing his hands together. Then came Frank and Lucy.

Jenny said, 'Mrs Brennan, why didn't you drive into the car park?'

Mrs Brennan said, 'Thunder doesn't like car parks. And it would have been better to have waited until summer to make this movie.'

Martin said, 'We want the movie to be finished by then so that we can show it

during the summer holidays.'

Mr Skelly, still rubbing his hands together, stepped forward. 'I am J. Skelly, the manager of the hotel. May I say, on behalf of my staff and myself, how delighted we are that you and ... and Thunder will be staying with us.'

'I'm Frank Johnson,' Frank said. 'I will be helping to write the script.'

'I thought the script had already been written,' said Mrs Brennan.

'Oh we've had some really very good new ideas since we arrived in Kerry. We are going to include them in the script,'

Jenny said very quickly. 'Now let me introduce Lucy Crater, who will be Betty Brannigan.'

'How do you do?' Lucy said.

'Not terribly well today. I have a headache but thanks for asking,' Mrs Brennan replied and attached a lead to Thunder's collar. 'We need to rest after the long journey. Where are our rooms?'

'We thought that the attics would be perfect for Thunder,' said Mr Skelly. 'Warm, dry, quiet, plenty of space.'

'The attics!' said Mrs Brennan. 'Thunder is not going to be put in the attics. He must be given his own room.'

The attics sounded just right to Flip and Flop. They gave two sharp barks.

'I think Flip and Flop might like staying in the attics,' Lucy said.

Mr Skelly beamed at the terriers. 'Yes, of course they would! Just as long as they don't break any plates like they did at breakfast.'

Everyone, except Mrs Brennan, laughed at this joke. She said,' I would like to see the new script for the movie as soon as possible. I hope there aren't too many other animals in it. Thunder doesn't like too many other animals around him.'

'That's not true ...' Thunder began to say but Mrs Brennan made him walk into the hotel before he could finish speaking.

'I feel sorry for Thunder,' said Flop. 'Mrs Brennan is *very* bossy.'

'Maybe you and I can do something about that,' said Flip.

'Just as long as we don't get into more trouble. Mr Skelly might change his mind about liking us, even though we did help to get him into the movie,' warned Flop.

'That is a chance we will have to take,' said Flip.

A warm wind blew across the yard, tickling the two terriers. Suddenly Flop no longer felt nervous. He chased Flip around the long car. Then Flip chased him around the humans.

Lucy said, 'Here comes Seamus. When he has finished unloading Mrs Brennan's car maybe he will show us these famous attics.'

5

Talking to a Dog Star

Seamus took the terriers' basket from room seventeen and carried it up to the attics. As he led the way he said, 'Some of the attics have been turned into bedrooms for people who work in the hotel. My own room is just here.'

He opened a door and the long gloomy corridor was filled with sunlight.

Flip and Flop looked into Seamus's room. It had a bed, and a dressing-table with a TV and a CD player on it. In the corner next to the bed there was a rail for clothes. Extra windows in the roof made the room very bright.

'It's very nice,' said Lucy.

'Flip and Flop will be next door so they won't get lonely,' Seamus said as he opened another door.

The room next door was still used to store things but all the boxes and pictures and books had been pushed against the wall. In the middle of the floor there was a brand new dog-basket. 'That was meant for Thunder,' Seamus said. 'Flip and Flop can use it now.'

'Bags first go,' said Flip and jumped into the new basket. 'Flop, you can try it later on.'

'How will Flip and Flop get out for walks and stuff?' asked Lucy. 'I may not be here all the time. And Frank will be working too.'

'Leave that to me,' said Seamus. 'I'll have a word with Mr Skelly. I will ask him if I can become the chief dog-walker.'

Flip and Flop liked the sound of that. They followed Seamus down to Mr Skelly's office. On their way past room sixteen they heard Mrs Brennan say to Thunder, 'This place is not fit for a star like you.'

Both the terriers thought that she was really thinking of herself and not of Thunder when she said that.

Seamus knocked at Mr Skelly's door.

'Come in, ' Mr Skelly said. He was still in a good mood. He listened to what Seamus had to say. Then he nodded his head. 'That is a very good idea indeed. Take as much time as you need to look after the dogs.'

Flip and Flop were delighted. So too was

Seamus, who said to the two terriers after they had left the office, 'Mr Skelly is a great friend of my father. That's why he gave me a job here. But I'm not very good at hotel work. Something always goes wrong. Mr Skelly keeps me on for my father's sake. But I like working with animals. Maybe now I will get a chance to prove that I can do something really well. Would you like to go for a walk?'

'Yes, yes!' barked the terriers.

'Your leads must be in room seventeen.'

When Seamus knocked at the door of room number seventeen, Lucy opened it. 'Mr Skelly said it is all right for me to look after the dogs. I'll need their leads to take them for a walk.'

Flip and Flop were about to go into the room with Seamus when they heard a snuffling noise under the door of number sixteen. 'That has to be Thunder,' said Flop. He and Flip put their heads against the bottom of the door. 'Is that you, Thunder?'

'Yes, it is,' came the reply. 'What are you and Flip doing?'

'Going for a walk with Seamus. Where's Mrs Brennan?'

'In the bathroom, combing her hair. When she's finished that, I think she is going to comb mine. Then she is going to lie down. She still has a headache.'

'Humans hate noise when they have headaches,' said Flip. 'Why don't you make a lot of noise? Bark and keen.'

'What good will that do?' asked Thunder. Flop was wondering the very same thing.

Flip whispered to Flop, 'Let's hide in the corner.'

The two terriers hid in the corner under a big armchair.

Thunder began to bark and to keen. It sounded terrible. 'No wonder he's a dog star,' said Flip. 'You would think that he was dying.'

And that was exactly what Lucy and Seamus thought. They ran out of room seventeen and banged on the door of room sixteen.

'What's wrong?' Lucy called out. 'Mrs Brennan? Thunder? What's wrong?'

'Maybe I should break the door down,' said Seamus.

'See if it's locked first,' said Lucy.

Before Seamus could do this Mrs Brennan

opened the door. Her hair was standing on end. Lucy and Seamus thought this was because she was frightened. Then they saw the comb in her hand.

'What on earth is going on?' demanded Mrs Brennan. 'Have you been upsetting Thunder?'

'Of course we haven't been upsetting Thunder,' said Lucy. 'He was making so much noise that we thought that you and he were in some kind of trouble.'

'Well we aren't in any trouble. But what could have made him carry on like that?' Then she saw the leads in Seamus's hand. 'It's your fault. You were rattling those leads.'

'He was not rattling those leads,' Lucy said very quietly and very firmly. 'I have only just given them to him so that he can take Flip and Flop for a walk.'

Thunder jumped up and down when he heard the word 'walk'.

'That's the truth,' added Seamus. 'Mr Skelly has put me in charge of all the dogs in the hotel.'

'A walk might do Thunder some good,' Lucy said. 'And you look as though you could do with some time to yourself.'

'Well I must admit that looking after Thunder is a great responsibility.' Mrs Brennan remembered that her hair was standing on end and tried to pat it into place.

'You could have some tea and lie down for a while,' said Lucy. 'Seamus will take good care of Thunder.'

Within minutes Seamus and the three dogs were down by the river. Thunder and the terriers had a great game of chase and crash. Then they sat down beside Seamus and had a talk.

'How did you get into the movies?' Flop asked Thunder.

'It was a bit of an accident really,' Thunder said. 'I was out for a walk with one of my humans.'

'Do you mean Mrs Brennan?'

'No, I didn't know Mrs Brennan then. The humans that I live with are called Mary and Paul. Paul loves to look at birds. During the fine weather he and I used to go to the Big Park to watch them. One day we were up there, sitting in the long grass, when we heard people shouting. We look-

40

ed up and saw a woman on a runaway horse. Paul and I ran after her. I got in front of the horse and forced the horse to turn around and stop.

'Then we found out that the horse hadn't run away at all. It was all part of a film that they were making! Paul and I were too far away from the camera to see it.'

'So then what happened?'

'Well they had to do the scene all over again, only this time they asked Paul if I could run after the horse again and pretend to stop it. Martin, who was directing the film, was delighted with the scene. So too was Harry, who trained the animals in the film. He will be here soon to show us what we are do in *Dogs*. He's a very nice man.

'Anyway to go back to that day in the Big Park, Martin got the idea of making another film with me playing a big part in it. The movie was called *Thunder, King of the Skies*. People all over the world went to see it. Then Jenny Lewis came over from America and asked Martin to make a movie with me in it.'

'How does Mrs Brennan fit into all this?' asked Flop.

'Paul and Mary have their shop to look after so they can't be with me all the time. Martin hired Mrs Brennan to take care of me. Usually she's all right but today she is in a bad mood because of her headache.'

'What happens to the money you get for being a dog star?' asked Flop.

'Paul and Mary are given that. And I am delighted because they are very good to me.'

'Do they take you for long walks?'

'Oh yes. They can afford a new car now

so we go to different places.'

Then Flip said, 'Do you know anything about the dead sheep?'

'What dead sheep?' Thunder asked. The two terriers couldn't help noticing that he shivered when he said the word 'sheep'.

'There are supposed to be dead sheep in the movie,' said Flop.

'That's the first I've heard of it,' said Thunder.

'We were wondering where they would come from,' said Flip.

Just then Seamus, who had dozed off in the warm sunshine, woke up. 'It's time I got you back to the hotel,' he said. 'Otherwise Mrs Brennan might be on the warpath again.'

'What kind of a path is a "war-path"?' asked Flip as Seamus put on their leads.

'I've no idea,' said Thunder.

When they reached the hotel car park, Silky was sunning herself on top of a van. 'I was wondering where you lot were,' she said. 'You're missing all the excitement.'

'What excitement?' asked Flop.

'James Brand and Gabriel Boyle arrived about an hour ago.'

43

'Who are they?' asked Flip.

'They are the human stars in the movie,' said Thunder.

'There are television cameras and everything here. They are looking for you. For the photographs,' said Silky.

'Mrs Brennan is going to be cross with Seamus for not coming back sooner,' said Thunder.

'Is Mrs Brennan the woman in room sixteen?' asked Silky.

'Yes, she is.'

'They took her away.'

'What do you mean "took her away"?'

'In an ambulance,' said Silky.

Mr Skelly looked out of a window. 'Where were you, Seamus?'

'I took the dogs for a walk. How is Mrs Brennan? Is her headache worse?'

'She has more than a headache,' said Mr Skelly. 'She has food poisoning. It's a good thing that she didn't eat anything here or the hotel would be blamed. You are going to have to look after Thunder while she is in hospital. Now come into the lounge and let Thunder meet some admirers.'

6

Dave Adams

Two famous actors, James Brand and Gabriel Boyle, were in the sitting-room. Reporters and cameramen crowded around them. The two stars stood up when they saw Thunder.

James smiled. The terriers had never seen such white teeth. He pointed at Thunder and said, 'Now here we have the real star of the film.'

'That's true,' said Gabriel. His teeth were as white as those of James but not quite so big.

'Are you pleased to be in the same film as Thunder then?' The question came from a young man standing by himself in a corner.

'Yes, of course we are,' said James.

'Some actors don't like working with animals,' the young man said. 'They think that the animals get too much attention. By the way, my name is Dave Adams. You may have heard of me.'

'Yes, we have,' said James grimly.

'What's going on?' Flop whispered to Thunder.

'Dave Adams writes for a newspaper in America,' Thunder replied. 'I have heard Martin talking about him. He is always trying to make trouble.'

'Who are these two dogs?' Dave nodded at the terriers.

'These are Flip and Flop,' said Jenny. 'They will be in the movie with Thunder.'

'No doubt they will be helping him to look braver than he actually is,' sneered Dave.

Martin stepped forward. 'Thunder has no need for anyone to help him *look* brave. He *is* brave.'

'That's not what I heard,' said Dave. 'I have been told that he jumps at the very smallest sound.'

There was a bang from a corner of the room. Everyone, including the dogs, jumped. Thunder slipped and fell. Dave pointed the small camera that he had hidden in his pocket at the dog star. He pressed the button. There was a huge flash like a great searchlight. It dazzled Thunder and the terriers and made them look as though

46

they were cringing in fear.

'That was a very nasty trick to play,' Jenny said. 'You asked someone to make that noise. Thunder wasn't the only person frightened by it.'

'It was just a chair falling over,' sneered Dave.

'Chairs don't fall over by themselves,' said Martin.

'Neither do brave dogs try to hide under tables when they hear a noise,' said Dave. 'So don't try and blame me if Thunder is a nervous wreck. See you around.' He pushed his way through the other reporters and out into the hall.

Jenny Lewis hurried forward. 'Ladies and gentlemen, this might be a good moment to introduce you to Harry, our animal trainer on the movie. If you want to know how brave Thunder is, Harry is the man to ask.'

Harry was a huge man. He had hands the size of shovels and arms like tree trunks. He was wearing a tee shirt with the words 'Animals Are Us!' written across it. 'Hello,' he said to Flip and Flop.

The terriers liked the sound of his voice.

Then he nodded to the reporters. 'I don't know where Dave Adams gets his ideas from but let me tell you this. I have worked with many animals on many movies. Thunder is, without doubt, the bravest dog that I have ever known.'

'Now then, time for some proper photographs,' Jenny said.

She had barely spoken when what seemed like a puff of white smoke moved across the room.

It wasn't smoke. It was Silky the cat. She sat first on James's shoulder and then on Harry's. Then she landed on Gabriel's lap. The photographers laughed and began to take pictures of the cat and the dogs and the human stars.

Flip said, 'Just wait until Bella and Slip and Slide see us in the papers. They will be very impressed.'

Poor Thunder didn't look very pleased. 'When the American newspaper publishes the photo that Dave Adams took, lots of people will think that I am a coward. They might not come and see the movie.'

'But the other reporters heard what Harry said about you being so brave,' said Flip.

'If they print that and show it on TV, it won't matter what Dave says.'

'He could make up all kinds of other stories about me,' said Thunder.

It was time now for the reporters and photographers and the TV people to leave the hotel. They were packing away their cameras and tape-recorders.

James said to Thunder, 'Don't let that creep Dave upset you.'

'That's right,' said Gabriel. 'He will soon get tired of making up stories about you. He will go back to America.'

'He's not staying in the hotel with us, is he?' James asked Mr Skelly.

'Certainly not!'

'Good!' The two human stars went out to look at the town and to say 'hello' to their many fans. The dogs looked for Silky but she was nowhere to be seen.

'Where's Thunder going to sleep while Mrs Brennan is in hospital?' asked Seamus. 'We can't leave him in number sixteen all by himself.'

'Could he not stay in the attics with Flip and Flop?' asked Frank.

'An excellent idea,' said Mr Skelly.

'That's settled then,' said Harry. 'Now where are the rest of the animals? I would like to meet them as soon as possible.'

'They live mainly at the farms by the sea,' said Lucy. 'I'll drive you out there if you like.'

The dogs followed the two humans out to the car park. 'Is this the first movie that you've been in?' Harry asked Lucy.

'Yes, it is! It's the first movie that Flip and Flop have been in too.'

'Making movies can be great fun but it is also very hard work,' Harry said. 'And talking of hard work, the sooner the animals and myself get down to it the better. That means an early start in the morning.'

Lucy opened the hatchback. The dogs jumped in.

'Thunder usually travels in greater style than this,' said Harry as he got into the front passenger seat.

'I know,' said Lucy. 'We saw the car that he and Mrs Brennan arrived in. It's as long as a railway carriage. It's parked in the yard. I thought that Dave Adams would be watching it to see if Thunder went anywhere. He would try to follow it. That's why I decided that we should go in my car.'

'Good thinking! Anyway Thunder seems to prefer this car,' Harry said. 'I don't know when I've seen him so happy.'

'That's because he has some dog friends now,' said Lucy.

The three dogs barked in agreement.

Lucy drove out of the town. The country-side sparkled in the bright sunshine. The islands and the sea looked like a painting. Even the O'Sheas' farmhouse seemed to be waiting to be photographed.

Jer came to meet the car. 'Hello, hello,' he barked. As soon as the terriers and Thunder were let out of the car they rushed off with him to the side of the house. Mitch and Topsy and Plucky, the wolf-hound, were waiting there to hear what had been happening. Silky was grinning down at them from the roof of a shed.

'How did you get out here so quickly?' asked Flip.

'Never you mind how I got out here so quickly,' purred Silky. 'I found out who knocked over the chair in the hotel. In fact I guessed that something was going to happen before anything did.'

Topsy said, 'Silky, would you mind starting your story from the beginning?'

'Not at all,' said the cat. 'It all started after I went back to the house in the market square that I share with Mrs Shannon. It cheers her up when she sees me and she always insists that I have something to eat. It's a good thing that I take so much exercise. If I didn't I would be as fat as a pet pig!'

'I've never heard of anyone keeping a pig as a pet,' said Flop.

'Oh they do,' said Mitch. 'There's a farm near the Lonely Pass and the humans there have two pet pigs called "Bacon" and "Ham". Fortunately for the pigs, the humans are vegetarians. But now go on with your story, Silky.'

The dogs settled down and listened to Silky.

This is what she told them:

As she slipped in through the kitchen window that was always left open for her, she heard Mrs Shannon coming down the stairs.

Mrs Shannon was saying, 'I don't us-

52

ually rent rooms but since you can't find anywhere to stay in the town, I'll rent one to you. How long will you be here?'

Silky looked out into the hall and saw Mrs Shannon talking to a man.

It was Dave Adams!

Dave said, 'About three weeks.'

Mrs Shannon was clearly surprised at this answer. She had expected to hear 'three days'. Before she could say anything Dave took a bundle of ten-pound notes out of his pocket and handed thirty of them to

Mrs Shannon, saying 'I just wish it could be more.'

The sight of so much money delighted Mrs Shannon. 'Oh please, this is more than I had expected. May I ask what you do for a living?'

'I write newspaper articles and take photographs. When I heard about the movie being made here I decided that there might be a good story.'

Silky said, ' I suspected that he was up to no good from the moment that I first saw him. He paid Mrs Shannon all that money in advance so that she couldn't ask him to leave if he caused trouble.'

'Could she not give him the money back?' asked Flip.

'Not now,' said Silky. 'There is a hole in the roof that needs mending. As soon as Dave left the house she arranged for Joe Dangle to come around and start work on it next week. That's where most of the money is gone.'

'I'll bet that Dave somehow found out that Mrs Shannon needed extra money before he asked her to rent him a room,' said Flop.

'You are right there,' said Silky. 'And I am pretty certain that information came from Corny Dunne, the town sneak. He'd do anything for money. I'll bet that he saw Dave Adams wandering around the town and thought, "Oh now, there is someone up to no good! Maybe I can help him."

'On my way back to the hotel I saw Dave Adams and Corny Dunne talking together in the doorway of the old cinema. I could tell that they were planning something. I didn't know exactly what it was going to be until someone knocked that chair over and we all jumped. It is my guess that the chair was knocked over by Corny Dunne. Dave Adams paid him to do it.'

'If Dave Adams has rented a room for three weeks, he is going to make more trouble for me,' said Thunder.

'What about the dead sheep in the movie?' said Flip. 'Do you think that Dave Adams might try and put the blame for that on us dogs?'

Nobody answered him.

7

Harry the Trainer

Harry, the trainer, whistled from outside the cottage. The animals hurried around to see what he wanted.

He was standing in the yard with Lucy and Mr and Mrs O'Shea. He counted the number of dogs. 'Six, including Thunder.'

'Don't forget Mitch, the donkey,' said Mrs O'Shea.

'And me,' said Silky. 'I might not get as good a chance as this again to show Harry what I could do in the movie! Harry didn't see me in the chase through the dining-room. I am sure that Mitch won't mind helping me. They might even end up calling the movie *The Cat and the Dogs*!'

She jumped on to Mitch's back. 'Okay, Mitch. Let's show them what we can do!'

Mitch kicked his heels in the air and galloped around the yard. Silky ran up and down his back. Then she hung on to his tail and swung through the air. Then she sat between his ears and put her paws over his eyes. That made Mitch come to a standstill.

'That,' said Harry, 'is one of the most amazing things that I have ever seen!'

Thunder said to the other dogs, 'If you don't do something Silky will end up as the second animal star of the movie.'

The dogs thought very quickly. 'How about pretending that we are rescuing Plucky from a fire?' suggested Flip.

Plucky ran into the farmhouse. After a few seconds he staggered to the door. He coughed. Then he fell backwards into the house.

Flip and Flop ran into the house and took Plucky's hind legs in their mouths. Then they dragged him out into the yard.

Topsy and Jer ran over and sniffed at Plucky, who didn't move. Then they looked at Flip and Flop, who pretended that they were too worn out to do anything else to help. Then Topsy and Jer jumped on to the wall of the farmyard, barked, and ran off to where Bart O'Sullivan was coming through the trees.

'I don't understand,' said Mrs O'Shea. 'What's wrong with Plucky? Why is he lying there like that? And why did Topsy and Jer run off like that?'

'There seems to be something wrong with Flip and Flop too,' said Mr O'Shea. 'Maybe we should send for the vet!'

Flip and Flop stood up and wagged their tails to show that they were feeling fine. Plucky did the same.

'Were they putting on an act for us?' asked Lucy.

'That's how it looked to me,' said Harry. 'They will be truly brilliant in the movie if they are that clever.'

Mrs O'Shea said, 'I hope they don't turn

out to be too clever for their own good. Now, Lucy, don't you want to show Harry the cottage.'

'I'd better go and see what Dave is up to,' said Silky.

'Try and find out something about the dead sheep,' said Topsy.

'I will,' said Silky. With a swish of her tail she was gone.

Next morning the first light of day had only just shone through the attic window when Seamus opened the door. 'Time to get up,' he said. 'Harry is going to start training you today for the movie. He is going to teach you to obey his signals.'

'That sounds like hard work,' said Flop.

'It *is* hard work but I will help you all I can,' said Thunder.

The three dogs ran downstairs after Seamus. Harry was waiting for them at the back door He gave them each a dog biscuit and a bowl of water. Then it was out to the yard. The three dogs looked around and were pleased to see that there was no sign of Dave Adams.

But Harry was taking no chances. 'We'll use the hotel van. Then if Dave Adams turns up later in the morning and sees that the long car is here, he will think that Thunder is still in the hotel.'

Just then the long car was driven into the yard. Pete, the driver, got out and said, 'Good morning. I hope I'm not late.'

Harry said, 'We weren't even expecting you.'

'Didn't you arrange for me to be called about fifteen minutes ago?'

'No, I didn't.'

'Well someone said that you did. I was still asleep when the phone beside my bed rang. A man's voice said that I was to be down here as quickly as possible to drive you and Thunder to where you wanted to go.'

'Was it an American voice?'

'No. The man sounded like one of the local people. I thought it might be one of the night staff phoning from the reception desk. Then there was the note from Mrs Brennan saying that Thunder is to travel only in his special car.'

'Who gave you this note?'

'It was left at the reception desk. I thought that someone from the movie company, who had been over to see Mrs Brennan in the hospital, left it for me.'

'And you are sure that the note was from Mrs Brennan?'

'I've never seen her handwriting but who else could it be from?' asked Pete.

The dogs looked at each other. The note could have been from Dave Adams. But who had phoned Pete just now, telling him to meet them in the yard?

Harry was wondering the same thing. 'Seamus, why don't you go and see who was on duty in the hotel last night? That person could have phoned Pete.'

'Okay.' Seamus ran back into the hotel.

'I wish you would tell me what's going on,' said Pete.

'We think someone is trying to hurt Thunder by writing bad things about him,' said Harry. Quickly he explained why he wanted to take the dogs in the hotel van.

Pete said, 'That puts me in a bad spot. If that note really was from Mrs Brennan I could lose my job for not doing what I was told.'

Seamus hurried back. 'I couldn't find anyone who was on duty last night.'

'In that case we had better do as the note says, in case it *is* from Mrs Brennan,' said Harry to Pete. 'The dogs and Seamus will go with you. I will meet you at the O'Sheas.' He got into the van and drove off.

Seamus opened the back door of the long car. Thunder and the terriers jumped in.

Flip and Flop looked at the lovely seats. 'Are we allowed to sit on these?'

'Of course, you are,' a very familiar voice said. It was Silky, the cat, curled up in a corner.

The dogs were about to ask her how she had got into the car. Then they knew that she would say, 'Never you mind how I got in here.' So they just nodded to her.

'Oh, so you don't want to talk this morning,' she said. 'That's a pity. I found out lots of things!'

'Such as what?' Thunder asked.

'Such as where the dead sheep are coming from,' said Silky. 'Mrs O'Shea is going to get them for the movie. I heard Martin talking to her on the phone last night. He asked her if she could let him have eight dead sheep. She said that she could.'

Flip said, 'But what exactly do they want the dead sheep for?'

Silky said, 'I know that too. I heard Frank and Martin talking about the script. One of the characters in the movie is called Whacky. He is a very wicked man. He does all kinds of terrible things like arranging dog-fights.'

'What do you mean?' asked Flop.

'It is a terrible thing that some humans do,' said Thunder. 'They train dogs to be very wicked and fierce. Then they put two dogs into a ring and let them fight each other. Often the dogs get very badly hurt. The man who owns the dog that wins gets a lot of money. Humans are not supposed to do it. The fights have to be kept very secret.'

'I have never known animals as fond of interrupting as the three of you are,' said Silky.

'Sorry,' said Thunder. 'Please go on telling us the story of the movie.'

'Where exactly was I?'

'You were saying about Whacky, the bad man in the movie, arranging dog-fights,' said Flop. Just to think of such a terrible thing made him shiver!

63

'Yes, of course,' said Silky. 'Now Betty Brannigan, that's the part that your Lucy has, suspects what Whacky is doing. However she can't prove it, so she goes and tells the man who works on the local newspaper about it.

'Now the name of the newspaper man in the movie is Conor Riley. Gabriel Boyle is taking that part. James Brand is going to be Whacky.'

'What happens then?' Flop forgot that he wasn't supposed to interrupt.

'Conor uses his own dog, that's you, Thunder, to try and find out where the next dog-fight is going to take place. At first Whacky thinks that Thunder is a stray and tries to make him wicked. Then he realises that Thunder is helping Conor. He tries to get him blamed for killing sheep.'

'They must be the dead sheep that Mrs O'Shea is going to get,' said Flip.

'Yes, they are,' agreed Silky, with a sigh at being interrupted yet again. 'Then after a lot of adventures and chases the truth come out. Whacky is arrested. Betty marries Conor and Thunder goes to live with them! It's what is known as a happy ending.'

'I wonder what exactly Flip and I are going to do in the movie, apart from running through the dining-room at the hotel?' asked Flop.

The long car stopped outside the O'Shea farmhouse. Pete and Seamus let the animals out. 'Where did the cat come from?' asked Pete.

Before she could be stopped, Silky ran over to where Harry and Jer and Plucky and Topsy were waiting. She jumped up on Harry's shoulder.

'Hello!' Harry said. 'I didn't expect to see you here.' Silky purred loudly into his ear. 'But now that you are here, you might as well watch while I put the dogs through their paces.'

'Yes, watch and learn,' Topsy growled at Silky.

For the next couple of hours the dogs worked very hard indeed, while Silky lay on a rock, enjoying the sunshine.

Harry made them crawl along the ground when he clicked his fingers. He made them sit up when he whistled. He made them run when he waved his left hand and stop when he waved his right hand.

He took them up and down the beach. Then he took them up and down the hill to the cave of O'Donoghue the Brave. When, at last, Harry let the dogs rest, Topsy said, 'This is worse than rounding up stray sheep.'

That reminded Flip and Flop to tell Jer about Mrs O'Shea and the dead sheep. Jer was as amazed as they were.

Silky, who had spent the last ten minutes chasing a lazy bluebottle, said,' I thought none of you were going to worry about any of that stuff.'

'It's easy for those with nothing to do to say things like that. And that's a well-known fact,' said Jer.

'Oh but Silky says she has plenty to do in the movie,' said Thunder. 'Isn't that right, Silky?'

'Yes, as you will soon find out,' snapped Silky. And that was all that she had time to say because Harry decided that the dogs should sit and watch while Silky and Mitch worked.

Harry made Silky jump from rock to rock. Then they all went back to the O'Shea farmhouse. Here Harry made Silky practise jumping off the roof on to Mitch's back.

Mitch didn't like this at all. 'She digs her claws into me when she lands on me,' he complained. 'I can't stand much more of it.'

Luckily there was no more for him to stand for Harry decided that they had done enough for one day. He told Seamus and Pete to take Thunder and the terriers black to the hotel. 'And the cat.'

But Silky had disappeared.

8

Detectives

The sign for the hotel had been taken down. In its place was a new sign in big letters: *The Ballydash News*.

'That must to be the newspaper office where Conor works in the movie,' said Flop.

'Is the hotel not a bit big for a newspaper office?' asked Flip.

'They will probably only use the front door,' said Thunder.

The dogs ran ahead of Seamus up the stairs. As they passed room number seventeen they heard a noise. Seamus said, 'Lucy must be in there. Let's say "hello" to her.' He knocked on the door. 'Lucy, are you in there?'

There was no answer.

Seamus tried again. Still there was no answer.

'There's no one there,' he said, but Flip and Flop now had the scent of a human in the bedroom. It didn't smell like Lucy. Whoever was in the room shouldn't be there!

Flip and Flop began to growl and then to

bark. Seamus understood what they were trying to tell him. He pushed the door open.

Flip and Flop rushed into the room ahead of Seamus. At first the room seemed empty. They ran to look out through the window in case the stranger had escaped that way.

As they looked out, the door slammed shut and the key was turned in the lock. Then they realised that the stranger had been hiding behind the door and had locked them in.

Even worse, Thunder was not in the room with them.

Seamus picked up the phone and dialled a number. 'Mr Skelly, this is Seamus. Someone has locked me and the terriers into room seventeen.'

Flip and Flop could hear Mr Skelly shouting at Seamus.

'It wasn't my fault,' Seamus said. 'Thunder is now alone on the landing.'

Those last words had a great effect on Mr Skelly. Within seconds he came rushing up the stairs. He unlocked the door and paused to catch his breath. Thunder came into the room.

'Did you see who locked us in?' asked the terriers.

'Just his shoes,' said Thunder. 'It all happened so quickly.'

'Could it have been Dave Adams?' asked Flop.

'He'd be afraid to risk being caught in someone else's room and accused of trying to steal something,' replied Thunder.

'Maybe it was the man who phoned Pete to meet us in the yard this morning,' said Flop.

'Will you all be quiet!' The dogs had forgotten that Mr Skelly was still there and was now speaking to them. 'Making all that noise!'

'There's no need to take it out on the dogs,' Seamus said.

'You are right. You are absolutely right,' Mr Skelly said. 'I just got a fright when you said that Thunder was by himself. I was afraid that he might have been kidnapped. How would we have explained that to Mrs Brennan?'

'I promise that I won't let Thunder out of my sight again,' said Seamus. 'By the way someone phoned Pete, Thunder's driver, early this morning and told him to meet us in the yard. Who was on duty last night?'

'Come down to the office and I will look at my list,' said Mr Skelly.

'What are we going to do?' asked Flip

'Maybe we should try our hands at being detectives,' said Thunder.

'What's "detectives"?' asked Flop.

'Detectives solve mysteries,' said Thunder. 'We will have to keep our ears open and our eyes peeled.'

'Do you mean peeled like a banana?' asked Flop.

In spite of being worried, Thunder had to laugh at Flop's question. 'No,' he said. 'I meant that we will have to be on the alert. We will have to look very carefully at everyone's shoes. Whoever was in the room was wearing black and white leather shoes with a red stain on them. If we find the person who is wearing those shoes, we will find the person who is helping Dave Adams.'

'But supposing the crook changes his shoes?' said Flop.

'That's why we have to find him now,' said Thunder. 'There's no time to waste.'

'If only we could get rid of Dave Adams,' said Flop. 'Then everything would be all right.'

'Things might get worse before they get better,' said Thunder. ' I might not be let go out with the two of you any more. Until we find out who was in Frank and Lucy's bedroom, all the humans are going to worry about me being kidnapped.'

Seamus came out of Mr Skelly's office. He looked very seriously at the dogs. He said, 'We still don't know who phoned Pete. Until we do, Thunder is more or less confined to barracks.'

'What does that mean?' asked Flop.

'It means that what I was afraid might happen, has happened,' sighed Thunder. 'I'm not going to be allowed out.'

'But you have to get exercise,' said Flip. 'And what if you want to piddle?'

'They will probably take me for walks around the yard,' said Thunder.

'That's no fun,' said Flip.

'Now it will be up to you and me to solve the mystery,' Flop said to Flip. 'And we are going to have to ask Silky to help us. I know that she can be annoying but she does find things out.'

Flip said, 'I'm surprised that Silky isn't here telling us what to do.'

'Maybe she is but we just haven't seen her,' said Flop. The three dogs looked up and down the shadowy corridor. There was no sign of the cat.

Seamus clicked his fingers at the dogs. 'I'd better take you all for a run outside. Then it's back upstairs for Thunder and me. I wonder where Lucy and Frank are. Mr Skelly wants them to make sure that there is nothing missing from their room.'

The dogs followed Seamus outside.

'Now then, I want no tricks from any of you,' said Seamus. 'Four times around the yard. Do your business. Then back inside until I get a chance to explain to everyone else what has happened.'

'Who's everyone else?' asked Flop, as he and Flip and Thunder started to sniff around the bins.

'Jenny and Martin and Lucy and Frank,' said Thunder.

Silky came strolling into the yard. She sensed that something was wrong and became as full of curiosity as only as a cat can become. 'What's going on?' she asked.

The dogs told her what had happened and asked her to help them. 'So now you want me to become a detective?' she said. 'That makes sense. Cats are born detectives. If things go well, Jenny and Martin might even decide to make a movie with me as star.'

A dreamy look came into her eyes. 'I can just see the posters now: *Danger in the Night* starring Silky, the wonder cat detective. But first things first and the first thing, as far as I am concerned, is to discover where Corny Dunne is. It could have been he who was in the bedroom. It is far too easy for people to walk in and out of this hotel.'

Seamus called out, 'Okay. Time to go back inside. Flip and Flop, you'd better come up to my room too until I speak to Lucy and Frank.'

'I don't suppose you know where Frank is now?' Flop asked the cat.

'He and Martin are working on the script in the big room near the bar,' she replied. Then she pointed with her tail to where Seamus was at the back door of the hotel. 'I think Seamus is having problems. First he gets locked into a bedroom. Now he seems to be locked out of the hotel.'

Silky was right. Seamus couldn't open the back door of the hotel. He tried one more time and said, 'We will have to go around to the front.'

The dogs followed him. Silky jumped over a wall and vanished from sight. Mr Skelly was at the reception desk, talking on the phone. He glared at Seamus. 'You have no need to come in this way.'

'Someone locked the back door,' said Seamus.

Mr Skelly spluttered, 'I don't believe it.

One thing after another. It is as though someone is trying to ruin everything.' Then he remembered that he was on the phone. He quickly said into the receiver, 'Oh I'm very sorry. I got interrupted.'

He listened to whoever was at the other end of the line. Then he began to splutter again but this time into the phone. 'Of course there is nothing wrong ... No, of course it has nothing to do with Thunder and the movie ... Thunder is right here beside me ...'

Seamus said, 'Mr Skelly, who are you talking to?'

'It's that American reporter, Dave Adams.'

'Let me talk to him.'

Mr Skelly handed the phone to Seamus, who spoke into it in a loud clear voice.

'Mr Adams? I'm Seamus Doyle. I am looking after Thunder and the two border terriers, who are in the movie with Thunder. They are in the very best of form.'

He listened for a few seconds. 'There has been no trouble of any kind. If there is any trouble you will be the first to hear about it, so why don't you write that down?'

As Seamus was speaking, Frank and

Martin came out of their office and listened as Seamus continued his conversation with Dave Adams.

Seamus was saying, 'Who do you think you are fooling, Mr Adams? I know that you are out to cause trouble. Now I have wasted enough time on you. Good-bye.'

Mr Skelly, his mouth wide open, took the phone back from Seamus.

Frank nodded admiringly. 'Well you certainly told him where to get off.'

Flip whispered to Thunder, 'Flop and I are going to slip away while Seamus tells Frank and Martin about someone being in the bedroom. We won't be very long.'

'Okay,' said Thunder.

Shoe Hunt

Flop followed Flip away from the reception desk. 'Where are we going?'

'To look for the man with the black and white shoes. The humans will be so busy talking that we will be back before they notice that we are gone,' said Flip.

The two terriers reached the swing doors into the kitchen. They had no trouble squeezing through them. The chef, who was stirring something in a huge saucepan, shouted, 'Get those animals out of here. Dogs are not allowed in my kitchen, not even movie-star dogs.'

A young man stopped rolling out pastry and tried to grab Flip and Flop. The terriers dodged under the long table in the centre of the room and ran up and down under it, looking at the workers' shoes.

Flop said, 'They are all wearing runners! Why would people who work in a hotel kitchen be wearing runners?'

'Maybe it's in case people don't like their food and they have to get away in a hurry,' said Flip. 'I think we might have to get away in a hurry as well. The man with the big white hat has a sweeping-brush.'

The man in the big white hat was, of course, the chef. He poked the brush under the table at the two terriers. 'Come out and get out,' he said.

The terriers jumped over the brush and made for the swing doors. Two waiters, arriving for work, stood by to let them pass. Flip slowed down to look at their shoes. Both waiters were wearing brown shoes. One waiter said, 'Those are the dogs that attacked Mr Skelly and stole the food yesterday morning.'

'Then they must be locked up,' the chef said. 'They are food crazy, a danger to me and my staff. Catch them before they get away.'

'We can't let Frank and Mr Skelly see us being chased again,' yelped Flop.

'Then the only way we can go is up-stairs,' answered Flip.

The terriers ran up the first flight of stairs, paused and listened. The chef and his staff hadn't seen them go that way. They rushed on into the reception area. There was a sound of angry voices.

'Hello! Where are you?' Thunder asked very quietly from the hall.

'We're up here,' Flop replied.

Thunder ran quickly up to the landing.

Flop said, 'Are the humans very cross with us? We were only trying to find the man with the black and white shoes.'

'The chef complained that you were in his kitchen looking for food,' said Thunder. 'But it's not what the chef said that's causing all the trouble. A fax of the article that Dave Adams wrote about me has just arrived from New York. He put in it that I am a coward and that that is the reason why the film script has to be changed.'

'Can't Jenny Lewis write back and say that isn't true?' asked Flop.

'It would be easier if we dogs could prove that the article is all lies,' sighed Thunder.

'You are forgetting that we supposed to be detectives now.' Silky was back again, slinking up the second flight of stairs. 'You have not asked yourselves why the back door into the hotel was locked just now.'

'I think that I know the answer to that,'

said Flip. 'It was done to upset Mr Skelly while he was on the phone to Dave Adams.'

'Which means that someone is watching us all the time.' Flop shivered. 'And whoever was watching knew that we were in the yard. That's how he knew when to lock the door. He must have then phoned Dave Adams on a mobile to tell him it was the right time for him to phone Mr Skelly.'

'They knew that we would come in with Seamus at that time and that Mr Skelly would say something that Dave Adams could turn it into something bad for his newspaper! Humans really can be very wicked,' growled Flip. 'And we still don't know who the man in the black and white shoes is.'

Silky said, 'Where would the human who locked the back door have been at that precise moment in time?'

'Inside the hotel, of course,' said Flip.

'And where did the three of you go when Seamus couldn't open the back door?'

'In through the front door, of course,' said Flop. 'You already know that.'

'Now, now, listen to me,' said Silky. Suddenly she acted as if she was playing a part in a movie. She began to walk up and down the landing. 'On entering the hotel by the front door, who did you see?'

'Mr Skelly ...'

'And no one else?'

Flop shivered again. 'I think I know what you are getting at. You are telling us that whoever locked the back door must still be in the hotel. He didn't go out through the front door. He would have been seen by the people at the reception desk. And the chef would never have let him go through his kitchen. But why didn't he unlock the back door and escape that way? He must have the key.'

'Perhaps he has some unfinished business upstairs; business that the two of you and Seamus interrupted a few minutes ago,' said Silky. 'Supposing he *is* back in Lucy and Frank's room looking for something right now, what are you going to do?'

'Catch him, of course,' said Flip.

'And how exactly would you do that? He could turn around and say that he had never been in the bedroom. He could turn around and say that he went upstairs by mistake. He could turn around and say that you attacked him. He could turn around and say that you are wicked, dangerous dogs.'

'If he turns around even once more I am going to get dizzy,' said Flip.

'We need a human to help us,' said Silky. 'We need someone like Seamus. I will be right back.' She jumped down into the hall.

She had no sooner vanished from sight than the dogs heard the sound of a bedroom door on the floor above them being opened. Quickly they scuttled into the dark corner of the landing. The shadow of a man appeared on the wall opposite the dogs. Flop began to shiver. So did Flip.

The man's shoes came into view on the stairs. They were black and white with a streak of red on one of them.

'That's him!' whispered Thunder. 'I recognise the shoes. He will get away if Silky doesn't come back soon with Seamus.'

The man didn't notice the dogs as he leaned over the banisters and looked down into hall.

'He's making sure that the coast is clear,'

whispered Thunder.

The man ran down the last flight of stairs into the hall. 'He's going to use the back door,' said Thunder rushing forward. 'We can't wait for Silky and Seamus!'

The two terriers and Thunder barked as loudly as they could and started down the stairs. The man managed to get the key into the lock and turn it. A crowd of humans, led by Seamus and Mrs Brennan, surged in from the reception area.

'When did *she* get back?' whispered Flop to Flip.

Mrs Brennan gave a loud scream when she saw Thunder about to run out through the back door.

'Where do you think you are going?'

She grabbed Thunder by his collar and glared at Seamus. 'I thought you were supposed to be in charge of these dogs.'

'I am in charge of them,' said Seamus.

'Well, you could have fooled me,' snapped Mrs Brennan. 'Thunder was about to run out there among cars and total strangers. Anything could have happened to him. No wonder Dave Adams can make up those stories.'

'How do you know what Dave Adam wrote?' Jenny Lewis demanded.

'Someone sent me a fax of his article to the hospital. Why else do you think that I got out of bed to come back here to see how Thunder was?'

'Pack your things,' Mr Skelly said to Seamus. 'This is all your fault. I want you out of this hotel at once. There is a bus to Killarney at four o'clock. I will phone your father and explain the situation.'

'That's not fair,' Flop said.

Flip said to Flop, 'Of course it isn't fair but we can't worry about that NOW. The crook is getting away.' He ran out through the back door into the yard. Flop ran after him.

10

Sniffing Around

Flop caught up with Flip at the next corner. They looked up and down the street. It was crowded with people and cars. There was no sign of the crook.

Silky appeared, as if by magic, from under a parked van.

'Where did you get to?' asked Flop. 'You said you'd bring Seamus back to help us catch the man in the bedroom.'

'I couldn't make him understand what I wanted.'

'It *was* the man with the black and white shoes. But we didn't see his face,' said Flip.

'Well, I know who it is,' said Silky. She was jumping from one parked car to the next. 'It's Corny Dunne. I saw him running out through the back door of the hotel. I'll bet that he has gone around to see Dave Adams at Mrs Shannon's house. I'll bet that Dave Adams is waiting there for the notebook.'

'What notebook?' asked Flop.

'The notebook that Corny had in his

hand when he left the hotel,' replied Silky. 'That must be what he stole from the bedroom. We have to get it back from Corny Dunne and Dave. Are you ready to cross the road?'

Flip and Flop looked out from among the parked cars. There was a gap in the traffic.

'NOW!' yelled Silky.

The two terriers dashed across the road.

'Down the lane,' Silky shouted. 'Down the lane!'

The two terriers ran down the lane in front of them.

'Keep going! Keep going!' Silky was running along the top of the wooden fence that lined one side of the lane. 'There's a loose plank just a short distance ahead. Can you see it?'

'Yes, we can,' panted the terriers.

'Then push through it to the other side.'

The terriers did as they were told and found themselves in a large garden that looked as if no one had tidied it for years.

'Where are we?' asked Flip.

'In Mrs Shannon's back garden.'

As they ran through the weeds and the

long grass, the terriers could not help noticing interesting smells.

'I wouldn't mind coming back here when things are a bit quieter,' said Flip.

'Neither would I,' nodded Flop. 'Do you think that things will ever get quiet again?'

Silky said, 'We can get into the house through the kitchen window. Mrs Shannon always leaves it slightly open for me.'

'What happens when we get inside?'

'We are going to do what all great animal detectives do,' replied Silky. 'We are going to start sniffing around.'

Silky had no problem with slipping in through the open kitchen window. It was more difficult for Flip and Flop. They had to wriggle and squiggle and push with their bottoms and arch their shoulders to open the window wider. Even then they barely managed to pop through it before it slammed shut with a BANG!

'Our tails could have been caught,' Flop gasped.

'Dave Adams heard that noise. He's coming downstairs to investigate right now,' said Silky. 'Nip in under the table. When you hear me say "Fresh fish" go into the

88

hall and hide under the stairs.'

Flip and Flop crept under the table.

Dave came into the kitchen. He looked around for any strange humans. Instead he saw Silky, who gave a big meow as if she was delighted to see him. Then she jumped off the table and landed on his face.

'Fresh fish,' she yelled. 'Fresh fish!'

'Get off, you crazy animal!' hissed Dave.

By the time Dave had rid himself of Silky, Flip and Flop were under the stairs. Silky waited until she heard the door of Dave's room close before she joined the terriers. 'Follow me,' she said. 'Time to go snooping upstairs.'

They ran up to the door of Dave's room and listened. Corny Dunne was talking in a very anxious voice. 'I don't care what you say. I heard something downstairs and it was not just that cat.'

'So how come that all I saw was the cat? It's always in and out of here,' said Dave.

'It's always in and out of everywhere,' said Corny. 'No matter where I go either it or those two terriers turn up.'

'They are just dumb animals and we are wasting our time worrying about them,'

snapped Dave. 'I have more important things to do such as copying down the things in this notebook. Then you have to get it back to the hotel before it is missed.'

'Go back to the bedroom in the hotel,' spluttered Corny Dunne. 'You must be joking! I've had enough narrow escapes as it is. I was almost caught by Seamus when I sneaked in this morning and used the phone to tell Pete to drive Thunder's car into the yard. Then you were too lazy to get up in time to follow them.'

'That has nothing to do with you. Just obey orders if you want your money,' warned Dave.

Silky and the terriers knew that it was time for them to have another chat. They slipped back down to the kitchen and in under the table.

Silky said, 'If Seamus could catch Corny Dunne in Frank and Lucy's room, I'am sure Mr Skelly would give him his job back.'

'Wouldn't Mr Skelly have to see Seamus catching Corny?' asked Flop. 'You yourself said that Corny could pretend that he had gone upstairs by mistake!'

'That's true,' agreed Silky. For the first time she looked really worried. 'Corny would have to be caught in the room by Seamus and someone else – with the note-book in his hand.'

'There is something that we have to figure out before we do any of that,' said Flop. 'How are we going to get away from here? The kitchen window is shut now. We'll never be able to open it.'

'And time is running out. Seamus might have left on the bus to Killarney before we can stop him,' said Flip. 'If there was another way out of this house, you could get Topsy and the others to come into the town and help us.'

'There is the hole in the roof that Mrs Shannon is going to have fixed,' said Silky. 'I suppose I could try to get out through that. It's not a very nice way out.'

'I know it's a rotten job but some one has to do it,' said Flop.

Silky nodded and began to talk like a TV detective again. 'Yeh, I guess you two hounds are right.'

They heard the front door open and the murmur of voices. Corny Dunne was leaving the house. He still didn't sound very happy at having to take the notebook back to the hotel. Dave sounded as bossy as ever. Then the front door was closed.

Seconds later Dave walked into the kitchen. He glared at Silky, who by now was on top of one of the cupboards. 'Cats! I hate cats almost as much as I hate dogs, so keep your distance while I make myself a cup of coffee.' He began to fill the kettle.

Silky slipped down off the cupboard, ran out into the hall and up the stairs. Mrs Shannon had piled all the furniture of the room, where the hole in the roof was, into one corner. The furniture was just high enough for Silky to use as a spring-board.

She measured the distance carefully with her eyes. Then she flexed her muscles, waved her tail and leaped forward. She managed to grab the edge of the broken slates with her front paws. She dangled in space. Then, with one final effort, she hauled herself out on to the roof. She looked beyond the town to the fields, the hills and the sea.

Like most cats she had very good eyesight and easily spotted Mitch, who was chewing away on the grass near the O'Shea farmhouse.

Quickly she moved to the roof of the next house. From there she made her way across the roofs of other houses and sheds until she reached the beginning of the countryside. Then, like a strange ghost blown by the wind, she followed the hedges until she was close enough for Mitch to hear her call out.

'We need help at the hotel. Call the others. There is no time to waste!'

11

Thunder to the Rescue

The closer he got to the hotel, the more Corny Dunne wished that he had never got involved with Dave Adams. He wished even more that he had never borrowed Frank's notebook, which was hidden inside his jacket. It seemed to get heavier with every step that he took.

He kept asking himself, 'How much longer will my luck hold out?'

Corny almost broke out in a cold sweat as he thought of the time he had spent hiding in Martin's study, listening to him and Frank talking about the movie script. If he hadn't told Dave that Frank had written it all down in the notebook, Dave would never have sent him to look for it.

He turned the corner. The hotel car park was so filled with cars that a van with the name of a radio station on it couldn't find a proper parking space. He tried the back door of the hotel. It was locked. The only way into the hotel was through the front door. The reception area was jammed with people. This would make it easier for him to go upstairs unnoticed.

He passed through the main lounge. It was crowded with reporters and photographers. There were TV lights and TV cameras.

'What exactly is happening here?' he asked a man

'Someone called Dave Adams wrote a story saying that Thunder, the dog star, is a coward! Now everyone wants to know the truth. There's going to be a press conference.'

For a second Corny felt like telling the man the truth of what had been happening. Then he became too afraid. He could be arrested for stealing the notebook. He pushed through the crowd and went upstairs.

He reached Lucy and Frank's bedroom. The door wouldn't open.

'It's locked!' thought Corny. 'All the rooms will be locked now to keep the wrong people out.'

There just had to be another way to get into the room. Then Corny remembered the sign for the Ballydash newspaper that the movie people had put up on the front of the hotel.

There had to be ladders somewhere around the hotel that reached that high. If he could find such a ladder he could maybe open the window to the bedroom from the outside.

If anyone questioned him he would say that he was cleaning the windows.

Corny pushed his way back out through the crowd and around to the old stables. That would be the place where ladders would be stored.

It took him a few seconds to get used to the dim light after the bright sunshine outside. The dust-filled air made him sneeze several times. When he stopped sneezing he saw exactly what he needed in the far corner of the stable. It was a long ladder that would easily reach the window of the bedroom. Even better, there were some folded overalls and a bucket in the same corner of the stables. He would have no difficulty in looking like a window cleaner.

He put on the overalls and made certain that Frank's notebook was tucked safely into them. Then he carried the bucket to the tap in the yard and filled it. As he turned to go back to the stables, a movement at one of the windows made him look up.

Thunder was watching him through the open window of Mrs Brennan's room. The dog's ears were pricked up as though he recognised him. Then a window in one of the attics opened. Seamus looked out. 'Have you seen two border terriers anywhere?'

'No. But when I've finished the windows I'll help you look for them,' said Corny. It was a good thing that Seamus was new to the town and didn't know who Corny was.

'Thanks very much,' said Seamus. 'But it might be too late then.' He looked at his watch. The time was three-thirty. The bus to Killarney would be leaving in half an hour. Then he would have to catch the train home and face his father.

He locked his suitcase and started downstairs. As he reached the next landing Mrs Brennan, with Thunder on a lead, came out of her bedroom. She paused when she saw him. 'Are you going somewhere?'

'I'm going home. Mr Skelly fired me.'

Thunder keened as though he understood what Seamus had said.

' Oh dear, I didn't mean that to happen. Maybe if I had a word with Mr Skelly we could work something out...'

'He's already spoken to my father, told him what happened. I am due home this evening.'

'And your mother?'

'My mother died when I was four.'

'Now I feel terrible. Absolutely terrible,' Mrs Brennan said.

Thunder licked Seamus's hand. Seamus stroked the dog's head. 'Good luck with the movie.' Then he ran downstairs and left his case at reception.

After all the noise in the hotel the main street of the town was very quiet but only for about ten seconds. Then there was total uproar as around the bend came Mitch, with Silky on his back, and, close on the donkey's heels, Topsy, Jer and Plucky. Behind the animals, waving a baton, came Garda Ryan. He shouted at Seamus, 'Head them off before they do untold damage. Stop the brutes! Stop the brutes!'

Seamus stood in front of the animals and

said very quietly, 'Easy! Easy does it!'

Mitch and the dogs barked, then turned and faced away from the hotel.

'Good lad yourself,' panted Garda Ryan. 'You halted them before they could get into the car park and maybe damage the cars parked there.'

'I don't think I've stopped them at all,' said Seamus. 'I think that they are off again. What's more, I think that they want us to follow them.'

Silky gave a meow of delight when she heard this and said to Mitch, 'For a human, young Seamus is very clever. We have to go back to the main street and down the lane behind the market square. Let's just hope that he goes on understanding what we want him to do.'

The animals had no need to worry about that. As soon as Silky and the dogs pushed their way through the fence into Mrs Shannon's back garden, Seamus followed them. Garda Ryan tried to do the same thing but he was too fat and got stuck.

Silky jumped up on the ledge of the kitchen window and knocked on it with her paw. Flip and Flop at once called out,

'We are still here!'

Seamus was delighted to hear the terriers. He quickly opened the window and let the two little dogs jump out into the garden. 'Now where do we go?' he asked.

'Back to the hotel,' said Flip. 'Dave Adams left the house fifteen minutes ago. He's up to something nasty. I think he was waiting until Corny Dunne put Frank's notebook back.'

There was a yell from the end of the garden. Garda Ryan had been pushed through the gap in the fence by Mitch. Unfortunately he had landed in a patch of nettles!

Seamus said to him, 'The animals are in a hurry. I think that I'd better stay with them. See you later on.' Then he ran down the lane after the terriers and their friends.

The animals did not stop until they reached the hotel. Mitch stayed outside to keep watch for Dave Adams. The cat and the dogs rushed into the hotel past Mr Skelly, who tried to stop them by throwing a guide-book at them. He yelled at Seamus, 'Now what are you up to? You will miss your bus.'

'That can't be helped,' said Seamus. 'This is more important.'

When Thunder saw Silky and Flip and Flop and the others arrive in the middle of the press conference he gave a loud bark that made Mrs Brennan scream.

Frank, sitting in the front row, said, 'Seamus, what's going on? I thought you were to keep Flip and Flop under control.'

'That was before I was fired,' said Seamus. 'These animals are trying to tell us something.'

'We are trying to tell them that Corny Dunne stole the notebook with the story of the movie in it,' Flop said to Thunder. 'Where's Dave Adams?'

'There's been no sign of him yet,' said Thunder.

'Trouble can often arrive later than it is expected,' said Jer. 'And that's a well-known fact.'

'Meaning that he must have gone some-where else first,' said Topsy.

'Exactly,' said Jer.

'There's been no sign of Corny Dunne either,' said Thunder, 'unless he's the man who said he was a window cleaner. Let's go out to the yard.'

'What's going on here?' Jenny Lewis pushed her way through the reporters, who had crowded around Frank and Seamus and the animals.

Seamus said, 'They want us to follow them.'

'They want ALL of us to follow them?' Jenny was stunned by the idea.

'It's just a trick to stop the truth from being told about this movie and this so-called dog star.' Dave Adams strolled into the room and waved a sheet of paper. 'This is the true story, which I have just faxed to my editor.'

'So that's what he was doing, sending more lies to America,' said Flop.

'Dead sheep! Sheep are to be killed to make Thunder, the so-called dog star, seem brave in this movie,' continued Dave. 'I read it myself in notes for the script.'

'Is this true?' someone asked.

'No,' said Seamus. 'It is not true and these dogs will prove it if we trust them. Let's follow them like they want us to.'

Outside in the hall, Mr Skelly stepped back in alarm when the cat and the dogs and the humans ran past him. 'Where are you going?' he asked. When he got no answer he ran after them out into the yard. The air was full of dust.

Flop said, 'Where's all that dust coming from?'

Flip said, 'The doors into the old stables are falling down!'

'Doors don't fall by themselves. And that's a well-known fact,' said Jer.

'Then someone must have done something to make them fall down,' said Topsy.

Thunder went on alert. 'I can hear a voice ...'

'So can I,' said Silky. 'It is Corny's voice from inside the stables. He is calling for help.'

'Stand back,' someone cried. 'The building is about to collapse.'

The front of the stables seemed to sigh. Then it fell down. Even greater clouds of dust rose into the air. People covered their mouths.

Thunder didn't hesitate before going into action. He rushed forward into the dust, with Mitch and the other dogs close behind. Silky sat on a window ledge and watched. Seconds later Thunder reappeared, dragging Corny Dunne by his legs. The crowd cheered and applauded. Cameras flashed. Reporters shouted questions.

As Frank and Lucy helped Corny Dunne to his feet, Frank's notebook fell to the ground. 'I have a confession to make,' Corny Dunne said.

Dave Adams, red with rage, stood on the edge of the crowd while Corny explained what he was doing in the old stable. 'I was hoping to use a ladder to get into Frank's room and return this notebook that I had been paid to "borrow" by a certain person. Not that I ever got any money from him nor would I take it now if he offered it to me. I think you all know who he is, without me having to name him.'

'But what made the stables fall down?' asked Lucy.

'I tripped while I was getting the ladder

out and it caught in the ceiling. The boards were all rotten. When I tried to pull the ladder free, the entire building started to collapse. If it wasn't for the bravery of Thunder, I could have been very badly hurt. Maybe even killed.'

'Three cheers for Thunder, the bravest dog in the movies,' called Gabriel Boyle.

'Forty-three cheers might be even better! And let's not forget all his animal friends,' said James Brand.

When the cheering stopped and all the pictures had been taken Dave Adams spoke again, 'Have you all forgotten about the dead sheep? If none of you believe me, why don't you ask Frank to let you see his notebook?'

'I've a better idea than that,' said Harry. 'Why don't we show you all the dead sheep out at the O'Shea place? Dave Adams, are you coming too?'

'No, I am not,' snapped Dave. 'I know what dead sheep look like!'

When they reached the O'Sheas' house Mrs O'Shea came out to meet them. Harry said, 'We would all like to see the dead sheep that are to be in the movie.'

Mrs O'Shea laughed. 'Oh would you indeed? Well I've put four of them out there on the side of the faraway hills. The others aren't ready yet.'

Everyone looked towards the faraway hills and saw what looked like four dead sheep.

'Dave Adams was telling the truth then,' a reporter said. 'You could end up in serious trouble with the The Irish Society for the Prevention of Cruelty to Animals.'

'I think you'd be better off phoning the Irish Association for the Prevention of Cruelty to Old Wool,' said Mrs O'Shea. 'That is what I made the dead sheep from – wool and some old rugs that I had stored this long time in the barn. No one making this movie would harm any animals. Neither would I nor anyone that I know.'

Everyone roared with laughter as they thought of how foolish Dave Adams would feel when he learned the truth about the dead sheep. By then it would be too late for him change his story. It would have already been published by the newspaper for which he worked.

12

Action and Happy Endings!

After the day of the 'dead sheep' every-thing began to move even more quickly. The weather became warm and sunny. There was very little time left for sitting around talking. Harry made the animals work very hard. The first scene they did was the chase through the dining-room. Before they began to act they were brushed and combed and had powder dusted all over their coats. The powder made them sneeze.

Harry stood behind the camera and give little signals and whistles, telling the animals what they had to do. They nearly always got it right.

It was Mr Skelly who had the problems. He was so nervous that, when it was time for him to act, he kept forgetting what he was supposed to do. When, at last, he did get it right everyone was worn out.

Seamus got his job back. Mr Skelly now wanted him to stay on at the hotel until the end of the summer. 'Then I have to think about going to college,' explained Seamus.

Jenny Lewis said,' Keep in touch. We can always use a bright guy like you on a movie.'

The human actors were very happy too. Everyone said that Lucy was going to be a big star. Silky was a bit cross that no one though that she going to be a big star too. But then she remembered all the photos of her that there had been in the papers. That made her feel very proud and content.

The day came when Thunder had to be kidnapped by the wicked Whacky. Everyone was so pleased by the way that Flip and Flop did their parts that they said they could be movie stars as well.

The humans were even more amazed at the way the dogs pretended that the fake dead sheep were real dead sheep.

'Gee what a bunch of mutts,' Jenny kept saying. 'They bring tears of joy to my eyes.'

The last days of the filming had Mitch and Silky raise the alarm about the dog-fight that wicked Whacky had arranged. Many of the people from the district, including Mrs Shannon and the O'Sheas, were in these scenes. There was a big chase through the woods on the faraway hills and then along the beach.

When Martin shouted 'CUT' for the last time everyone was suddenly sad. Then Jenny said, 'Okay, folks! The work is over. Time to play. We are going to have a party.'

And what a party it was! Long tables loaded with food and drink were put out in the yard of the hotel. Music blared from loudspeakers. Everyone in the town turned out. Soon, not only the hotel yard but the streets were crowded with laughing, dancing people.

The animals gathered in the car park and watched.

'I will be leaving tomorrow,' Thunder said.

'Does that mean we will never see you again?' Flop asked.

'Of course you will,' said Thunder. 'There is going to be a special showing of the film to raise money for the ISPCA. They are going to invite all of you to it.'

'To a cinema?' said Silky. 'A donkey and a gang of dogs going to a cinema to look at a film? Now if it was only me, I could understand it!'

Just then Jenny Lewis came out to get something from her car. She shrieked when she saw all the animals together. 'I've just had another great idea for a movie. *The Car Park Pack.*'

Forgetting why she had come into the car park, she ran back to the hotel. 'Frank! Martin! Harry! I've just had a great idea for another movie.'

'If she gets any more movie ideas she'll be here until next summer and that's a well-known fact,' said Jer.

'Maybe we can think up some titles ourselves,' grinned Flip. '*Five Dogs Need Help*, followed by *A Bark in the Dark*, followed by *Sheep Can't Dance.*'

'Followed by a happy ending for everyone,' said Flop.

The dogs began to laugh so much that the humans came to see what was going on.

This is the fifth Flip 'n' Flop book. The others are:

Flip 'n' Flop

The two border terriers come from Scotland to start a new life with Frank in the Wicklow hills … and have a moment of high drama when the floods come.

More about Flip 'n' Flop

The terriers move to Killiney Bay, go swimming and fishing and exchange gossip at the local vet's. But they have problems with the cat next door, and Frank's father just doesn't seem to like them.

Adventures with Flip 'n' Flop

The terriers learn about dog-doors and have an exciting walk when they meet foxes and badgers. Then the Indian summer comes to a stormy end and they face their biggest challenge.

Flip 'n' Flop in Kerry

The terriers move to Kerry, where they meet Topsy, a sleuthing sheep-dog intent on solving the mysterious disappearance of Plucky the wolf-hound. Last seen yesterday and now vanished into thin air.

All £2.95

TONY HICKEY is one of Ireland's most popular children's writers.

For The Children's Press he has also written the *Matchless Mice* series; *The Black Dog*, set in his native town of Newbridge, County Kildare; *The Castle of Dreams*, which has been turned into a musical and performed in Bermuda; *The Glass Globe Adventure*, involving dosh-raising to buy a crystal globe; and *Granny Learns to Fly*, in which Granny Green, tidying up her attic, makes an astounding discovery which completely changes her life.